Amelia Bedelia's
• First Valentine •

Have a heart, Amelia Bedelia!

By Herman Parish
Pictures by Lynne Avril

Greenwillow Books
An Imprint of HarperCollinsPublishers

For my Uncle Clarence
a valentine for a Ballentine—H. P.

To Herman, Virginia, Sylvie,
and Bernadette—love, L. A.

Amelia Bedelia's First Valentine. Text copyright © 2009 by Herman S. Parish III. Illustrations copyright © 2009 by Lynne Avril. All rights reserved. Manufactured in China. For information address HarperCollins Children's Books, a division of HarperCollins Publishers, 195 Broadway, New York, NY 10007. www.harpercollinschildrens.com

Gouache and black pencil were used to prepare the full-color art. The text type is Cantoria MT.
Amelia Bedelia is a registered trademark of Peppermint Partners, LLC.

Library of Congress Cataloging-in-Publication Data: Parish, Herman. Amelia Bedelia's first valentine / by Herman Parish ; illustrated by Lynne Avril. p. cm. "Greenwillow Books."
Summary: Literal-minded even as a child, Amelia Bedelia muddles through Valentine's Day with her heart on her sleeve, trying to make sense of strange greetings at school and home, and ever on the look-out for the arrows of Cupid.
ISBN 978-0-06-154458-3 (trade bdg.)—ISBN 978-0-06-154459-0 (lib. bdg.)—ISBN 978-0-06-154460-6 (pbk.)
[1. Valentine's Day—Fiction. 2. Schools—Fiction. 3. Family life—Fiction. 4. Humorous stories.] I. Avril, Lynne, (date), ill. II. Title. PZ7.P219Aqf 2009   [E]—dc22   2009009050

15 16 SCP 10 9 8 7   Greenwillow Books

Amelia Bedelia saw hearts everywhere. She spied them in the sky, spotted them at the park, and even found them on her french fries. She was surrounded by love.

"Mom, where are you?" Amelia Bedelia yelled
when she got home from school.
"I'm in the living room!" Amelia Bedelia's mother
was playing cards with her friends.
Amelia Bedelia loved to play cards, too. She peeked
over her mom's shoulder.
Hearts! A whole handful of hearts!

"Wow!" Amelia Bedelia said.
"Look at all those valentines!"
Her mother's friends laughed.
"Amelia Bedelia," said her mother.
"Don't tell them what I'm holding!"

"You're holding cards, Mom,"
said Amelia Bedelia. "Anyone
can see that."
Amelia Bedelia's mother handed
her a brand-new deck of cards.
"Here—a present for you.
Now skedaddle. Your snack is
in the kitchen, cupcake."

Amelia Bedelia couldn't find any cupcakes in the kitchen, just a plate of brownies. She grabbed one and sat down at the table. She put her new deck of cards in her knapsack. She liked them, but she didn't really need them. She already had a bunch of cards to finish before the Valentine's Day party at her school tomorrow.

Amelia Bedelia's teacher, Miss Edwards, had made cards
for everyone to decorate at home. Amelia Bedelia got right
to work. Many of the cards confused her, so she did her
best to fix them.

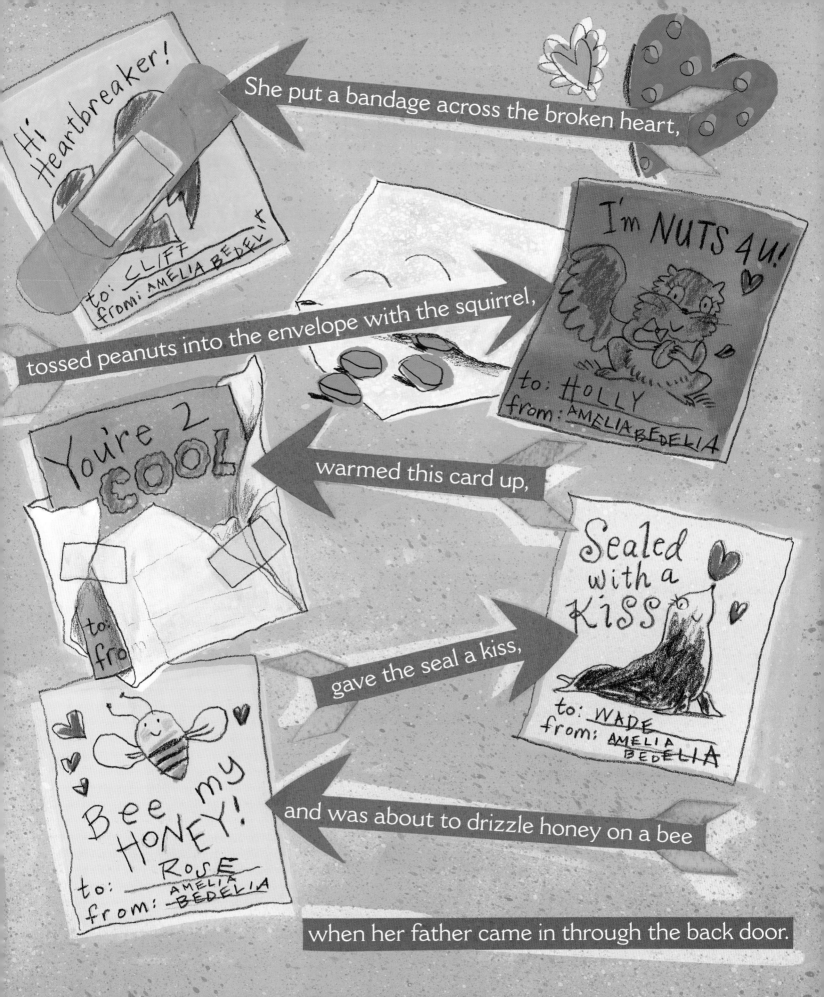

"Hey, Daddy!" she said. "Did you know that tomorrow is Valentine's Day?"

Amelia Bedelia's father kissed her on the top of her head. "So your mother has reminded me every day this week," he said with a chuckle. "Tell me something I don't know."

Amelia Bedelia thought for a second, then said, "Teddy lost a tooth at recess."
Her dad smiled. "Teddy is lucky," he said. "He'll get a visit from the tooth fairy tonight, and a visit from Cupid tomorrow."
"Who is Cupid?" asked Amelia Bedelia.

"Cupid is a little baby with wings," said Amelia Bedelia's father.
"He flies around on Valentine's Day and shoots arrows at people
when they least expect it. If his arrow hits you, then you'll fall
in love with the next person you see."

"What!" yelled Amelia Bedelia.
"Don't tease me, Daddy. Babies don't have wings."

"It's a myth, not a joke," said Amelia Bedelia's father. "Now, what should I get for Mom—candy? Flowers? Jewelry?"
"Yes!" said Amelia Bedelia's mother. "I'd like all of the above."
Amelia Bedelia looked up. All she saw above was the light on the ceiling. Why would her mother want that for Valentine's Day?

That night, Amelia Bedelia had the most amazing dream. Cupids, hearts, and candy kisses swirled around her. "I'm nuts for you!" squeaked a giant chocolate squirrel. Fuzzy sugar bees floated through the air.

Bee my honey

I'm nuts for you!

When Amelia Bedelia
woke up the next morning,
she was still a bit sleepy
and she was late.

She jumped
into her
clothes,

wolfed down her
breakfast,

blew her
parents a kiss,

and raced for the bus,
quick as a whistle.

"Come on, slowpoke," the bus driver called. "You're holding us up!"
"That's impossible," Amelia Bedelia said. "I'm not strong enough!"
She climbed on board and tucked the special Valentine's Day cards
under her seat so they wouldn't get crunched.

The Valentine's Day party started right after lunch. There were decorations and games and tons of treats. There was a giant cake baked in the shape of a heart and an enormous bowl of fizzy pink punch.

"Can I have a little punch, please?" asked Clay.

Amelia Bedelia gave him a little punch on his arm.

"Owwww!" yelled Clay.

The other kids laughed. Amelia Bedelia did not.

She was too busy keeping an eye out for Cupid and his arrow.

At last, it was time to exchange Valentine's Day cards.
That's when Amelia Bedelia remembered what she had forgotten.
Her cards were still on the bus.

Amelia Bedelia was miserable.
"Amelia Bedelia, you are wearing your heart on your sleeve,"
said Miss Edwards. "What's the trouble?"

Amelia Bedelia looked at both of her sleeves. She saw stripes, but no hearts.

"I don't have cards for my friends," she said. "I left them on the bus." She put her head down on her desk. She started to cry.

The whole class gathered around Amelia Bedelia.
"Here's what we'll do to make everyone feel better," said Miss Edwards,
patting Amelia Bedelia on the shoulder. "Let's get busy. Everyone please
pick an activity. You can make your own heart box, play Pin the Heart
on the Skeleton, or I can show you a card game called Hearts."

"I have an idea!" shouted Amelia Bedelia. She looked at Miss Edwards and smiled. She wiped her eyes. She opened the deck of cards her mother had given her. She took out her markers.

"It's okay," announced Amelia Bedelia a few minutes later. "I've got valentines for everyone!"

Later that afternoon, Amelia Bedelia found her valentines on the bus, right where she had forgotten them. She was thrilled. She leaped off the bus and zoomed down the sidewalk. She held the heart box she had made at the party up to the sky and twirled around and around and around and . . .

"Bull's-eye!" yelled a boy, as he jumped out of the bushes.

The boy was Jeremy, and he lived on her street.
She'd known him since she was a baby.
"I am not a bull, Jeremy," she said. "And this is not an eye!
You could have broken my heart!"

"I don't want to break your heart, Amelia Bedelia," said Jeremy. Amelia Bedelia didn't believe him.

"Cross my heart," he said, as he really crossed it. "Was school fun today? My mom made me stay home because I was sick this morning."

"You missed Valentine's Day?"
asked Amelia Bedelia.
Now she felt sorry for Jeremy.
So sorry that she decided to give
him all of her special cards.

"Here. Happy Valentine's Day,"
she said.
"Thanks," he said, walking
away. He turned and blew her a kiss.
Amelia Bedelia made a face. She
sure didn't love him, but there was
no reason not to like him.

When Amelia Bedelia's father got home, Amelia Bedelia and her mother gave him a box of chocolates.

He presented a bouquet of flowers to Amelia Bedelia's mother and a bracelet to Amelia Bedelia. The bracelet sparkled and a tiny pink heart dangled from it.

"Thank you, Daddy," said Amelia Bedelia.
"Now I can wear my heart on my wrist
instead of my sleeve."

"Hug time!" shouted Amelia Bedelia's father.
"Double hug time!" shouted Amelia Bedelia's mother.
"Triple hug time!" shouted Amelia Bedelia.

It was the greatest family hug ever.
And Amelia Bedelia wished they could stay
just like that until next Valentine's Day.